Beneath the Poet's Sky

By

Edward Lee McDaniel Jr.

For permission requests, write to the author, addressed to:

Edward Lee McDaniel

TABLE OF CONTENTS

My Mellow Yellow Bird!

My mellow yellow bird is a cockatiel.
He loves it when I talk to him.
We share ideas and build.
He let me know if he approves.
He nods his head to say yes.
Shakes his head to say no.
He's happy as long I'm around.
him in the room, he gets upset
when I have to go.
We are like two peas in a pod.
We bring out the best in one another.
He's more than a bird to me he's my brother.
He is always chirping, keeping my spirits high.

He makes me laugh when I'm
upset and want to cry.
If I don't give him some
attention, he will protest and
make a lot of noise.
He wants just as much
attention as the rest of my
home girls and home boys.
He loves it when I read him
poetry.
He's quiet and calm, you won't
hear a peak.
If I skip reading to him, he will
squawk and squeak.
He loves my writing he is my number one fan.
He doesn't like being ignored and
put on the back burner; that's what he can't stand.
My mellow yellow bird sitting in his cage.
He's happy if I perform for him on our private stage.
He's my best buddy; he has my utmost respect.
He won't let anyone stick their hand in his cage; he will peck.
All my mellow yellow bird wants is lots of attention, love, and affection.
I look at him and I see my reflection.
I am him and he is me.

This is dedicated to you, my mellow yellow bird.

This is your piece.

You've helped me appreciate the simple things in life we all have a role,

and we all play a part.

I'm glad you are a part of my life.

I love you from the bottom of my heart.

When I Look

Into

The Mirror ...

I glimpse reflections of moments in life's flow,

In the mirror's gaze, my story on display, I know.

A man with flaws, yet strength and beauty here reside,

Against all odds, a determined heart, with pride.

From the day I was born, my parents' love did bloom,

Through light and darkness, they saw me as a blessed plume.

A way with words, the gift of gab I've found,

Talents aplenty to uplift those who are bound.

A gentle giant, helping hands extend with grace,

Guiding elders across streets, ensuring their safe embrace.

A teddy bear's heart, a lion's roar, both in me blend,
Injustice and cruelty, to my core, I can't pretend.

If a genie granted one wish, oh, the world I'd implore,
No one should suffer, pain and
hardship nevermore.

In this mirror, I see love for all that I
am,
My uniqueness, curves, and spirit like
a soothing balm.
A heart of gold, each spoken word a
guiding star,
Touching souls deeply, no matter near
or far.

In kindness, I believe, in treating
others fair,
Sometimes misunderstood, but it's a cross I'll bear.
Eyes reflecting my soul, intentions pure and true,
Changing what I can, accepting what I can't undo.

Blessed to be here, among the living, I see,
I've been through much, but I stand free.
Though I may not look like the battles I've been through,
I'm still here for a reason, there's much more to do.

To see everyone rise, succeed, and shine,
In this mirror's reflection, I find layers, yours and mine.
Strengths and frailties, vulnerabilities to embrace,
Displayed for the world, in this poetic space.

Proud of my beauty, unashamed of my flaws,
In this mirror's light, I find a greater cause.
Not perfect, just human, this I understand,
In the mirror's reflection, I see a complete man.

Now, as you gaze into your mirror's glow,
Accept every facet, let your self-love flow.
Love the good and the bad, in your unique grace,
In this mirror's embrace, let your soul find its place.

Choose Love Today

Love heals all wounds, it's true,
Chasing dark clouds, making skies so blue.
Love is action, not just a word to say,
It proves itself in deeds every single day.

Love can unite, crossing party lines with grace,
Opening eyes, making hearts change their pace.
Cherishing people, valuing every dime,
Love teaches us to use our precious time.

Love can bring nations close, not pull apart,
Fixing economies, easing inflation's dart.
Together we stand, a united team,
One heartbeat, one goal, like in a dream.

Today's a perfect day, let love abound,
Hug your kids, and
spread kindness all
around.
Compliment strangers, be
selfless indeed,
Less greed, more
gratitude, plant that seed.

Treat others kindly, as you
wish to be,
Love's what the world
needs, can't you see?
To make our world a brighter space,
Choose love today, and hate will erase.

Speak

To Me

Through Your Poetry

Hey, fellow poets and sisters too,

Speak to my soul, let your poetry break through.

Empower me with your lyrical might,

Show me your vision, paint it so bright.

Share your strengths, inspire with flaws,

Be a fearless warrior, wield those poetic laws.

Ink your words bold, make emotions ignite,

Speak to my heart, let your verses take flight.

Your mission, poet, is to reach beyond the known,

Creativity's canvas, a world of your own.

It's more than words on paper, don't you see?

Bring them to life, let your spirit run free.

Give me goosebumps with vivid scenes you create,
Honesty and transparency, don't hesitate.
Wrap me in stories, make me feel so
alive,
Connect to your truth, help me
survive.

I want to see what you've seen,
feel what you've felt,
Join your journey, let my
heart melt.
Emotional rollercoaster, take
me high and low,
Leave me breathless, let your
emotions flow.

Make me laugh, make me upset, make me cry,
Lead me through life's maze, reach for the sky.
Leave it all on the page, set fire to the stage,
Your words will echo, they'll never age.

Craft that piece, spark endless debate,
You shut it down, your words resonate.
Spit that fire, make me reminisce,

Your poetry's power, I won't dismiss.

So speak to my heart through your poetic decree,

Make me remember when you spoke to me.

I Am A Man

I'm just a man, can you see?

Deserving fairness on this land, like you and me.

I've been down, won't follow the devil's plan,

No longer fooled by schemes, I take a stand.

I'm just a man, seeking love and peace,

Spreading kindness, let all hatred cease.

Not your stereotype, not what you might think,

I'm someone's son, someone's bond, in life's link.

I'm just a man, with talents deep inside,

Moving mountains, shaping life's tide.

Love's the answer, problems at hand,
I know my worth, I deserve the grand.

I'm not perfect, a work in progress
still,
Accept me as I am, or let me
fulfill.
Love me in my flaws, as in
perfection's view,
I'll stand by your side, just like
you should do.

We all make mistakes, we all have
our slips,
Forgive me as I forgive, love in our grips.
Learning from our errors, seeking a better way,
I'm just a man, doing my best every day.

No superpowers, no cape or grand plan,
Just a regular man, like any in the clan.
Doing my best, from dawn to dusk's span,
Remember, in the end, I'm just a man.

Poetry Is From the Heart & Soul

Poetry springs from heart and soul's embrace,
Speak your truth, let your spirit trace.
Still waters run deep, in verses they keep,
Awakening masses from slumber's sleep.

Blank canvas, words as your artful brush,
Let your voice resound, in every hush.
Poems written, to poetry they aspire,
Spoken word, igniting a passionate fire.

A purpose greater, we often don't perceive,
Dreamers yearning the credit we'll receive.
A mind is precious, don't let it go to waste,
We craft our art in a safe, creative space.

Imagination guides us, agents of change,
Escapism's allure, we beautifully arrange.
Verbal masterpieces painted with care,
Pen's touch ignites adrenaline's flare.

Creative writing, my first love, my crush,
Content matters, in the world we hush.
High hopes soar, glass ceilings can shatter,
We state our names, proclaiming our matter.

One community, united we stand,
Spitting messages, reaching the land.
Not all will grasp, but some surely will,
To see what's possible, you must shoot your skill.

The poet's evolution, like a butterfly's flight,
Baring the soul, tears in the night.
When poets depart, angels cry above,
Their words endure, an everlasting love.

Poetry's sustenance, food for the mind,
Nourishing the soul, to life it's aligned.
In the heat, it's a cooling breeze,

In the cold, a warming tease.

Meek and humble, yet bold at times,
Raw and unapologetic in poetic rhymes.
When conversations falter, and friends aren't near,
Notebook and pen, your voice is clear.

Here, you're free, your thoughts unfurled,
Uncompromised expression, your inner world.
Things unsaid in daily chatter's drill,
In verse, they flow, expressing your will.

Words, a gift, freedom's embrace,
Sometimes a curse, sometimes a grace.
Encouraging, inspiring, empowering, too,
Affirmation in verses, a lifeline for a few.

In desperation's hour, words find their place,
Revelations emerge, a saving grace.
Positive motivation, a guiding light,
Through dark times, in poetry's flight.

Voices of reality, poets speak the real,
Ink their pain, hoping others heal.

Born

And

Made A Poet.

The day I became a poet, let me unveil,
Spitting bars, a lyrical warrior's tale.
Crafting words and verbs, a vivid display,
Creating explicit pictures in a unique way.

Like a twisted voyeur, through eyes I'd peer,
No filters, a double-edged sword, crystal clear.
Anyone who crossed my path felt the heat,
In Helena town, talent's test, a challenging feat.

Hard times, racial lines, job prospects thin,
People turned cold, as the ice would begin.

Too many paid the price, following the trend,
Mimicking songs and movies, a bitter end.

It's a shame, they never learned
their worth,
Valuing human life, a lesson
from birth.
Wasting energy on hate and
tearing down,
With plenty for all, there's no
need to frown.

Casualties of a war, too late
they'd wise,
That's why I take poetry seriously, no disguise.
It's more than an art, it's a heartfelt mission,
Life lessons delivered, heed their transmission.

Why cancel each other, let's build instead,
Stop the killing, release the hate we've spread.
Like apples and trees, we're not far apart,
Better examples we should be, from the start.

Life's a mix, bitter and sweet in its beat,
I take it to the page, my words like a beat.
Carrying the torch for legends gone before,
Paving the way for us, they opened the door.

In the age of narcissism, I find my way,
Avoiding the abyss, where darkness may sway.
A long, winding road, I signed up to tread,
Urgently sharing my message, or I'd explode instead.

Spitting a piece before an audience's gaze,
Setting the bar high in those earlier days.

Words That Bring People Together

The day I became a poet, let me unveil,
Spitting bars, a lyrical warrior's tale.
Crafting words and verbs, a vivid display,
Creating explicit pictures in a unique way.

Like a twisted voyeur, through eyes I'd peer,
No filters, a double-edged sword, crystal clear.
Anyone who crossed my path felt the heat,
In Helena town, talent's test, a challenging feat.

Hard times, racial lines, job prospects thin,
People turned cold, as the ice would begin.
Too many paid the price, following the trend,
Mimicking songs and movies, a bitter end.

It's a shame, they never learned their worth,
Valuing human life, a lesson from birth.
Wasting energy on hate and tearing down,
With plenty for all, there's no need to frown.

Casualties of a war, too late they'd wise,
That's why I take poetry seriously, no disguise.
It's more than an art, it's a heartfelt mission,
Life lessons delivered, need their transmission.

Why cancel each other, let's build instead,
Stop the killing, release the hate we've spread.
Like apples and trees, we're not far apart,
Better examples we should be, from the start.

Life's a mix, bitter and sweet in its beat,
I take it to the page, my words like a beat.
Carrying the torch for legends gone before,
Paving the way for us, they opened the door.

In the age of narcissism, I find my way,
Avoiding the abyss, where darkness may sway.

A long, winding road, I signed up to tread,

Urgently sharing my message, or I'd explode instead.

Spitting a piece before an audience's gaze,

Setting the bar high in those earlier days.

The Fire Inside Me

A burning fire deep within, that's me,
Motivating, striving for the poet I aim to be.
A hunger for success, hidden from plain view,
Mere mortals can't perceive what drives me to pursue.

If you can't handle the heat, it's best to retreat,
Deceitful souls, you won't defeat.
Prayers for my downfall, I simply delete,
Find another place, have a comfy seat.

My pen bleeds in the lab, where I create,
Spitting fire, feeling complete, don't hesitate.
I aim to impress, primarily, just me,
But in this game, competition's decree.

Beauty and the beast, we coexist,
Then it's time to feast, don't resist.

Can I find peace in this endless strife?
Loose lips clapping, but what's the price?

In this game, clout without money is hollow,
Like faith without works, it's tough to follow.
All in good fun, until someone's hurt,
Some poets seem great, but real life can be curt.

Not everyone gets their
flowers in the living,
Unnoticed efforts, it's a
shame, unforgiving.
A lifetime's toil often goes
unsung,
Credit due in life, not after
we're done.

Why wait till they're gone to give acclaim?
Why let their hourglass empty, it's not the same.
This game can chew and spit you out,
Moving on to the next hype, no doubt.

Don't bark louder than your bite, be strong,
In a rhyme fight, you'll need to belong.
Poets wedded to the mic, heart and soul,
Pouring it all out, for a higher goal.

Critics tough, these streets are rough,
Calling your bluff, it's not enough.
If my best falls short, show me the way,
Define dopeness, let's agree or sway.

Cross the line, awaken a giant, take heed,
I may disagree, but accept the message, indeed.
Not my time to shine, lesson learned in kind,
The fire still burns, success I still bind.

Maybe it's a wall I keep trying to ascend,
Falling down, but I'll crawl till the end.
When I emerge from my corner, stand back,
Firing on all cylinders, on the right track.

Today, a lesson, for all to discern,
Don't play with fire, or you might just burn.

What Good Is A Pen Without Ink

A pen without ink, what's its worth?

Like a poet without words, a loss since birth.

A building without structure, a purposeless space,

A lighter without fire, a meaningless chase.

Telling your truth, accused of a liar's feat,

Don't shoot the messenger, don't penalize the beat.

A cow without milk, a chicken without eggs,

A heartless man, devoid of love's pledges.

A car lacking steering wheel, engine, battery,

A person with flattery, but nothing to see.

A pen without ink, like a restaurant stripped bare,

A church void of members, an unanswered prayer.

A man who can't think, lost in the maze,
A purposeless person, wandering through days.
A radio, silent, with no sound to be found,
This too shall pass, a pen without ink I've found.

Imagine a movie, no pictures,
no sound,
A life of existence, not living,
tightly wound.
A playground, children
absent in the sun,
A creative community where
no building's begun.

A mind wasted, a terrible, sad
haste,
Think before you act, don't let it go to waste.
All inspired by a pen with no ink to link,
In its emptiness, a message to think.

You're

Still A King

You're Still A Queen

McDaniel, hear the truth, let it ring,
You're still a king, you're still a queen.
Even when they treat you like a pawn,
Ignore your voice, like you're just a pawn.

You're still a king, you're still a queen,
With determination, you can achieve the unseen.
Don't let them steal your self-esteem,
You have every chance to live the American dream.

Ignore the hype, disregard the lies,
In your own narrative, let your spirit rise.
From beginning to end, your story you'll mend,

You can do anything, my dear friend.

No diagnosis or disability defines your way,
Let nothing or no one lead you astray.
You're still a king, you're still a queen,
Unleash your potential, let your essence gleam.

You don't have to conform
to their call,
Only answer to yourself,
stand tall.
You're still a king, you're
still a queen,
Believe in the Most High,
let your faith be seen.

With persistence and hard
work, you'll achieve,
Don't let negativity hold you, believe.
Leave behind those doubting voices, so unkind,
Others' opinions won't define your mind.

Let your radiant light inside brightly shine,

You're still a king, a queen so divine.

If you set your mind, you can achieve anything,

Ignore those who say you can't, let your spirit sing.

Stop

Taking Things

For Granted

Every day we wake, let's be thankful, it's clear,
Seeing the sun, hearing the rooster, hold them dear.
In the land of the living, we're here to stay,
Release grudges, put beefs aside, today.

Differences aside, let's make amends,
Forgive, for ourselves, make amends.
Life, people, nothing's guaranteed,
No one owes us, God provides what we need.

Time borrowed, spend it wisely, be kind,
Actions matter, in this world, we're defined.
Here today, gone tomorrow, in a blink,

Life's fragile, let's cherish every link.

No guarantee for the next second's delight,
Cherish each moment, both
day and night.
Commute to work,
shopping, no promise
there,
Blessed with a roof, clothes,
food to share.

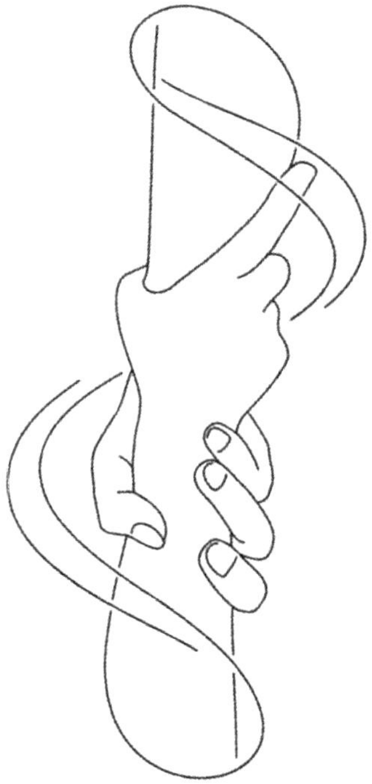

Foolishness abounds,
judgment's not the way,
We've all faltered, at some
point, lost our way.
Don't drag others when we
have our own past,
Forgiveness, the key, let judgment be cast.

God forgives us, so why can't we, too?
Wasting time on arguments, what's the value?
Let's grow up, act our age, be adults,

Getting along is a must, end the insults.

Some things left unsaid, could avoid the strife,
Using our heads, the key to a better life.
Living our best life, every single day,
Confident in our choices, come what may.

Man enough to apologize, when we're wrong,
Words don't define us, it's actions that belong.
Character speaks volumes, that's what we see,
In these trying times, let love set us free.

Pray for the world, pray for America's grace,
Burning bridges, we may need to retrace.
Not every smile's a friend, let's not pretend,
Actions reveal true selves, in the end.

What's done in the dark, eventually shows,
Each day we step forward, letting our hearts compose.
We're awesome on purpose, let that be clear,
Never let d isagreements linger, let's steer.

Tomorrow's not promised, make amends today,

Time borrowed, never taken for granted, we say.

Everything for a reason, God knows the way,

Let's love one another, make this our day.

My Beautiful Blackness

My blackness shines, so beautiful to see,
I'm phenomenal, unique, and truly me.
I silence negativity, it's irrelevant to my soul,
When I speak with intelligence, I take control.

Moving mountains and crowds with every word,
Verbal healing, like a song from a bird.
I bring hope to the hopeless, that's my grace,
Life's my muse, in its embrace, I find my place.

No matter the odds, I stand firm and strong,
Focused, determined, all day long.
Like a Phoenix, I rise from the ashes anew,
Every challenge faced, I come through.

I'm not a stereotype, I'm a work of art,
Unique and deep, with a warm, beating heart.
Greatness and chaos within, it's true,
A poet's job is never done, I pursue.

Breaking barriers in a world filled with sin,
Hate or love me, I continue to win.
In my beautiful black skin, I'm secure,
I am astrology, science, and so much more.

Universal, divine, my essence so bright,
My abilities awe, yet they spark some fright.
A king, I roar, for love, not war,
Evil may try, but I'll settle the score.

Scientists may plot, seek our decline,
But we'll rise like stars, through every time.
Struggle runs deep, in my bloodline's flow,
My beautiful blackness will continue to glow.

Try and try, but never hold me down,
I'm a force, a beacon, a king with a crown.

In the face of adversity, I proudly stand,

My beautiful blackness, forever grand.

Let's Shine The Light On Love

And

Dim The Light On Negativity

Treat others as we want for ourselves, it's the key,
Amidst the doom and gloom, we won't let it decree.
With will and way, we'll find our stride,
Taking back control, starting today, with pride.

Let's do better, for ourselves and the human race,
Chase the dark clouds, let the sun embrace.
Empathy for the unfortunate, a kind word to share,
On a higher frequency, like birds in the air.

Uplift one another, let positivity prevail,
If no good can be said, then let silence sail.
Send positive energy to those who've hit the ground,
Don't revel in their troubles, let compassion resound.

Together we stand, divided we fall,
Each action ripples, affecting us all.
To make this world better, we must start within,
Be the change, let the healing begin.

Learn from nature, the wisdom of
the trees,
Time for peace, let conflict cease.
More love, less hatred, fewer beefs,
More empathy and understanding,
for lasting relief.

Be humble, not grandstand, it's the
way,
Kindness and compassion, let them
hold sway.
In this together, no room for being mean,
No 'I' in 'team,' in unity, we glean.

At this turning point, our vibes find our tribe,
On a higher frequency, we must imbibe.

Shine light on love, dim negativity's view,
Reverse the cycle, for a dawn anew.

These troubles won't last, they too shall pass,
Joy arrives in the morning, like a looking glass.
Love, harmony, like the solar system's grace,
In proper setting, time, and space.

Taking back control, it starts in our minds,
In darkness, seek the light, that's what binds.
Dark clouds dissipate, with love's gentle strife,
Spread love, speak life, and embrace a better life.

When I Look Into The Mirror

When I gaze into the mirror's embrace,
I see reflections of my life's entire race.
In this image, I see a man of flaws and grace,
Strength and beauty, a determined face.

Born of a love that was strong and true,
My mother and father, blessings anew.
A young man, gifted with words and more,
Offering hope to the lost, like never before.

A gentleman, aiding the elderly on the street,
No discomfort, no need to retreat.
A gentle giant, injustice my roar,
If granted a wish, suffering no more.

I cherish my curves, in my unique design,
A heart of gold, moving souls every time.
Treating others as I wish to be treated,
Kindness sometimes misunderstood, yet undefeated.

Looking in my eyes, windows to my soul,
Good intentions guide me, filling my role.
Blessed to be here, still in
the land of the living,
My past doesn't define
me, it's the journey I'm
giving.

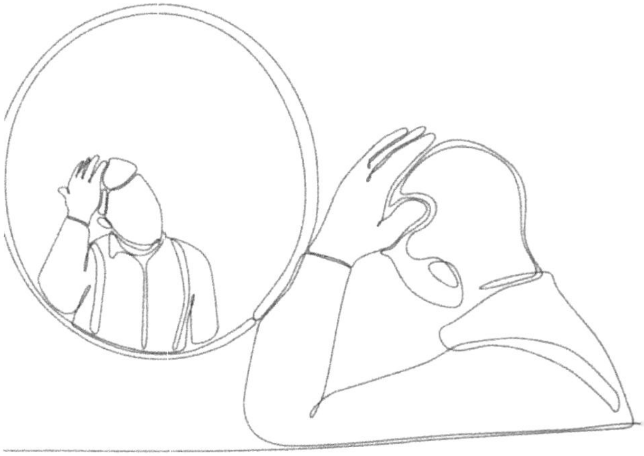

I want to see everyone rise
and succeed,
In the mirror, I see all that
I need.
Strengths, weaknesses, vulnerabilities all there,
Proud of my beauty, owning my despair.

I'm not ashamed of who I am, you see,
Accepting every part, both the beauty and ugly.

Through Christ, I believe, I can overcome,
Though my actions may baffle, I'm not done.

I'm a sweet person, yet not perfect in hand,
Just a man, trying to understand.
Now, when you face your own reflection's light,
Embrace every measure, day and night.

Love your good side and the not-so-bright,
Perfect and imperfect, both in sight.
Embrace every inch, every pound and line,
In the mirror's gaze, let your self-love shine.

Only You Can Quench My Thirst

I want you now I can't hold it in any longer
You are trying to resist this temptation
It only makes me come after you stronger
I want to make your rivers run again
I can tell you are going through a drought
I want to unlock your sacred mysteries
I want to see what you are about
You appear in front of me like a mirage
But I know your body is real
I want to have complete carnal knowledge of you
I want to give you something you can feel
Only you can put out this deep burning desire
I want for the both of us to explode together
I want us to rub our bodies together
Causing sparks that set a fire

I like what I see your body is tantalizing
Why you have to play hard to get
Why fight the feeling with the stroke of my hurricane tongue?
I can get you soaking wet I know what you want
And you have what i've been needing
I want to engage in the art of
karma sutra with you
All of your expectations I'm far
exceeding
Why you have to be so mean?
Why you have to talk all that
trash?
I want to beat it up like a drum
I want to wax that ass
It's human nature you were made
for loving
Your body was made for exploring
Anything else is not living it's just existing
I want to make your flood gates start pouring
This kind of passion I'm talking about Is like war and peace
Only you can extinguish this fire
Only you can tame this beast

Only you can quench my thirst

So why you want to leave me stranded Sexually frustrated in heat?

Sometimes I get jealous of the chair

Because it gets to rub up against your seat

We need to explore the law of physics

My mass pressed up against your density

I want to unlock your sacred doors with my master key

Test out your engine and listen to your motor run nice and smooth

We need to get together and do what we need to do

I want to do it so well we both fall fast asleep

Let Big Ed show you how I stroke the kitty and make it purr

Use my hands and my magic stick to go deep

What are you waiting for?

This is a gift to be received.

It's not a curse.

You are the only one who can quench my thirst.

Let It Marinate All Over Me

Time has treated you with such grace,
Let's celebrate this beautiful embrace.
I adore your silky-smooth, bronzed skin,
As it simmers gently in a pot, within.
On the stove, it cooks low and slow,
In its natural juices, the flavors grow.
Let's savor this moment, let it marinate,
Your soul aglow, like honey's sweet fate.

If I could, I'd whisk you away,
On a magic carpet, we'd sway.
I'd bring a fresh red apple, a sweet bet,
To become your teacher's cherished pet.
In dreams, we'll craft a night to remember,
Sopping up gravy with biscuits tender.
Stirring around, like cake batter divine,
Together, we'd cause an earthquake to align.
I wish to see you dance like Beyoncé,

Shimmy and shake, in your own way.
You've aged so gracefully, my dear,
Like vintage brandy, cherished and clear.
Snow on your peaks, fire in your valley,
Tasting like cotton candy, my sweet
finale.

But it's all a fantasy, a delightful
game,
Let it marinate in passion's flame.
Take it slow, with our hearts in sync,
As we dive into passions, let our
thoughts link.
With a brush, I'll paint on your
canvas, free,
Exploring your depths, like the vast
sea.
Until I uncover Atlantis, my quest so grand,
You're my classic automobile, my Catalina, so grand.

On your ice track, we'll slip and slide,
Bringing joy like lottery wins, side by side.
I long to break your levee, set you free,
Let your waters flow, wild and carefree.
Let it marinate, my love, let it bloom,

In this sweet, passionate, romantic room.

You and I, together, a perfect fate,

Let it marinate, my love, don't hesitate.

Happy Anniversary My Love

After all these years, the flame remains,
Burning bright with love that never wanes.
I remember the day we first did meet,
At a friend's birthday party, our paths did greet.
Our journey together, it started that day,
And our love has blossomed in every way.
As a power couple, side by side,
Our love empowers, like a rising tide.

God's blessing, so divine and true,
When He brought me someone like you.
In 2003, it became official, our bond so tight,
Husband and wife, in love's sweet light.
Happily married, like peas in a pod,
A special bond, protected by God.
We live life fully, come what may,
With you by my side, it's a sunny day, always.

Four children now, as we celebrate twenty years,
God sent an angel to calm our fears.
Wine tasting, Greece trips, and birthdays galore,
Our love's special, that's for sure.
Lakers and Cowboys, our teams apart,
But united in love, you've
captured my heart.
Both Christians, joy and
happiness we deploy,
What God joined together,
nothing can destroy.

True love is a treasure, a
beautiful thing,
In this journey together, we are
king and queen.
After all these years, my heart
still sings,
I knew from the start; you were
the real thing.
True love, they say, comes once in a lifetime,
I promised God, you'd forever be mine.
Through prayers and staying hand in hand,
You turned my cloudy skies to blue, you understand.

I'm willing to travel to the ends of the earth,
With you, every adventure holds its worth.
Each day, I thank God from deep within,
For a love that's true, a love that's a win.
You, my everything, my sweetheart so true,
Happy 20th anniversary to the one I love, it's you.

I Say I'm Ok

But I'm Not Okay

It was a late summer afternoon.

The sky was a strange orange then angry grey and black.

The thunder was crashing, the lightening was flashing.

The heavy rain begins to hit the rooftop and pound against the concrete.

The ground was already saturated.

The streets began to flood,

The same way my mind does some nights on my pillow as I lay,

My tormenting thoughts have me tossing and turning.

Will this storm ever go away?

How do I go on living this way

I say I'm ok but I'm not ok

I'm damaged but not broken

Eyes wide shut

Eyes wide open

For acceptance and understanding

I am hoping

You tell me to be more vocal

I was taught to be careful what I say

Truth is I'm not ok

Denying I have a problem

Won't make it go away

I bare this burden every day

It's complicated my brain freezes

I forget the words to say

These tormenting thoughts don't go away

The war wages on inside my head

Another day

How do I go on living this way

I say I'm ok but I'm not ok

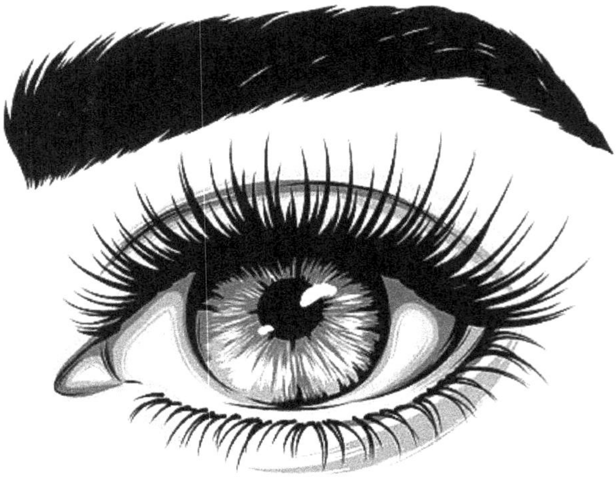

I Wish Heaven Had A Phone

I really wish that heaven had a phone,
So I could speak to my loved ones who have flown.
I remember my mother and father's sage advice,
"Keep your head up," they'd say, always so nice.
"God won't give you more than you can bear,"
Through life's cards dealt, they taught me to care.
No matter the odds, hold your head high and be strong,
Even when everything feels like it's going wrong.

When it seemed like the world was falling apart,
My parents told me to trust God from the heart.
"Don't be discouraged," they'd lovingly advise,
"Young man, hold on," as they dried my tearful eyes.
In these times, we lean on God's mercy and grace,
Yet, some who speak ill once smiled in our face.
In this world of noise, everyone wants to be heard,
But only a few take time to listen, it's absurd.

Clout chasing, struggling, trapped in poverty's grip,
People compete when they should peacefully coexist.
Sometimes, I prefer to keep my thoughts concealed,
Holding emotions in isn't a healthy shield.
On those Sunday dinners, Mom's
love would shine,
Turning me from feeling low to
feeling fine.
She'd remind me that I'm
destined to be a winner,
While Papa read stories that
made my dreams grow bigger.

I cherish the moments I shared
with my dear folks,
Wish I could discuss current
events and jokes.
I'm sure they'd say, in their wise and caring way,
"Our world is astray, let's find the right path today."
God's will shall prevail, we must trust and obey,
He'll make a way, even when skies are gray.
To my parents and ancestors watching from above,
Rest in love, dear Mom, Dad, and all, with hearts full of love.

Cherish

I often have thoughts in the back of my mind

Wondering why there are some things you never find.

I came to the conclus.on it's all about faith

If you only believe you would

be surprised what can take

place

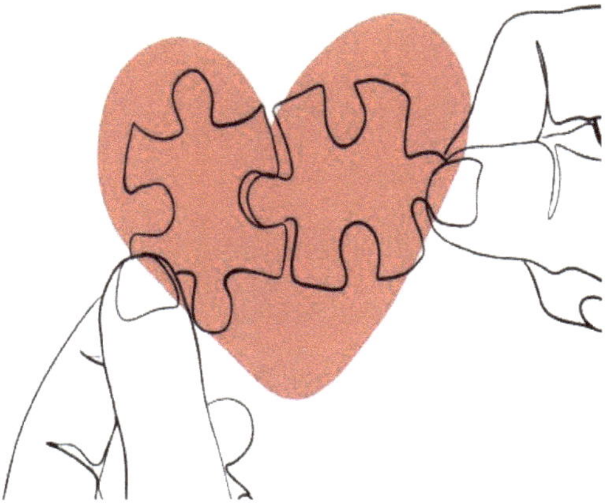

Life is a gift from our

heavenly creator

We should cherish what we

have now

Not worry about later

In life no ones perfect yet me strive to be the best

We end up failing life's simple tests

Too many judges and not enough humble civilians

Children honor your mother and father

Parents stand by your children

I can't go back

I can reminisce

I never imagined my life would come to this

Remembering a time, I was young, wild, and free

When there was nothing but time on my side

I thought it was all about me

Mom and dad said there would be days like this

I was like a little kid in a candy store

I couldn't get enough of that sugar crisp

If you knew me back then you would say oh brother

I would get myself out of one sticky situation and into another

I had good intentions, somehow, I always found trouble

The people I used to hang out with

The things I did

All now are just water under the bridge as I reminisce

Looking back at person I used to be

It's quite amazing how the road turned

As I remember the many times I got burned

I had to bump my head many times before the lesson was learned

I was out of control young naive and didn't care
It's truly a blessing from God that my life was spared
I can't go back to those ways, but I can reminisce
I made it through that journey in my life
I'll make it through this
I can't go back but I can reminisce.

Life is not always a walk in the park

In the depths of darkness, we must be cautious,
Cherishing both day and night, it behooves
us.
For what's hidden will eventually come to
light,
In self-love, we find strength to win the fight.
Treat others kindly, as you'd wish for yourself,
Love's a gift, a treasure on life's intricate
shelf.
It grants us wings to soar, like a gentle dove,
In this world of delicate creatures, it's love we
all covet.
Sometimes, we lose our way, wander astray,
A simple word of encouragement can brighten the day.
Just as flowers crave water and gentle care,
Each soul needs a touch of kindness to bear.

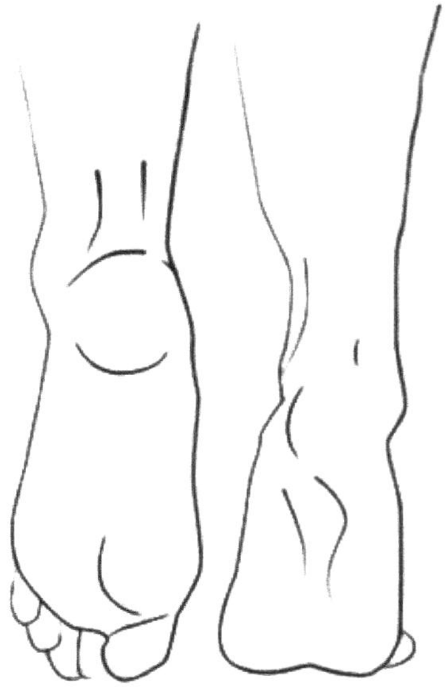

I Rise

If you take away my hands
I would still write
If you take away my voice
I would still speak
I still rise I will never concede to defeat
My soul is deep
If you take away my Twitter account, I'll still tweet
I march to the drum of my own beat
Every attempt you make to silence my voice
I turn up the heat
You knock me down
I get back up on my feet
You can take me off all of social media
I will still find another platform to speak
You are not the first
You will not be the last person in the world
That has tried to take something away from me
The depth of the measure of this man is far more deep
Then mere mortal's eyes can see
I don't fear man or woman
Only God can stop me

Like that tree planted by the riverside
I shall not be moved
You are doing something right when dogs start barking
Dogs bark at objects on the move
When you are a force to be reckoned with
Everything but the kitchen sink gets thrown at
You to try to stop you
You will be falsely accused of saying things you did not say
You will be falsely accused of doing things you did not do
Some of your friends will align with your enemies
Start plotting against you
New levels new devils
I will be alright I will still rise when the dust settles
It's something about when I speak the truth that cuts deep
It's a problem when you are trying to liberate people
Who don't want to be liberated
When you progress, they want you to regress
I still rise for those who see the best out of my worst

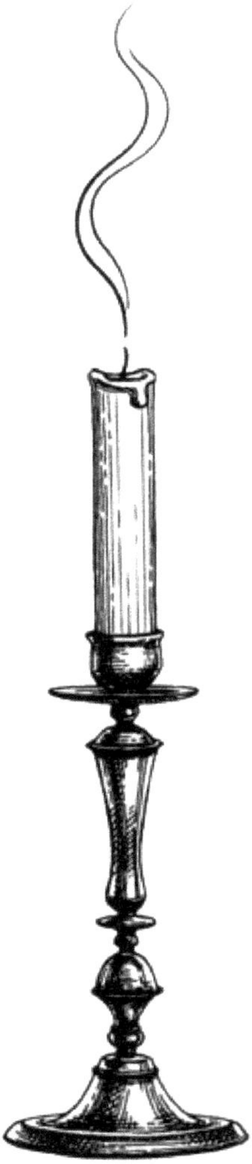

I rise for those who see the worst out of my best

I rise in the face of the people who have my back

I rise in the face of those who sneak attack

One door closes a new door opens

I will never stop believing in myself

I will never stop creating masterpieces

I will never stop hoping

I will continue to raise awareness

I will keep my eyes open

Even on my darkest days

I will search for the light at the end of the tunnel

Even when I stumble

I will get back up on my feet and rise again

This is not the end

It's only a new beginning

I Have Some Learning To Do

I've realized I have much to learn,
To stop letting others' words and actions burn.
I won't let negativity consume my soul,
For it drains my energy, taking its toll.
I find myself wanting to escape, to sleep,
Shutting down for weeks, emotions running deep.
You ask where I've been, what's going on with me,
I've been recharging, setting my spirit free.

I'm becoming aware of the world's effect,
How people and the environment can intersect.
Mental health tied to what we consume each day,
It's crucial to prioritize in every way.
Taking breaks is okay, don't hesitate,
Refresh your mind, don't let it stagnate.
Amidst clutter, confusion, and life's noisy stew,
Find time for yourself, this is overdue.

Work on self-improvement, a vital goal,
Engage in self-
evaluation, make
yourself whole.
Seek a tranquil space,
practice your breath,
You're the captain of
your ship, guiding its
path.
Don't overload your
vessel, lest you flip,
You can't be
everything to
everyone, don't let it
grip.
We often prioritize
everything but
ourselves,
Make self-care a priority, for it restores our inner wells.

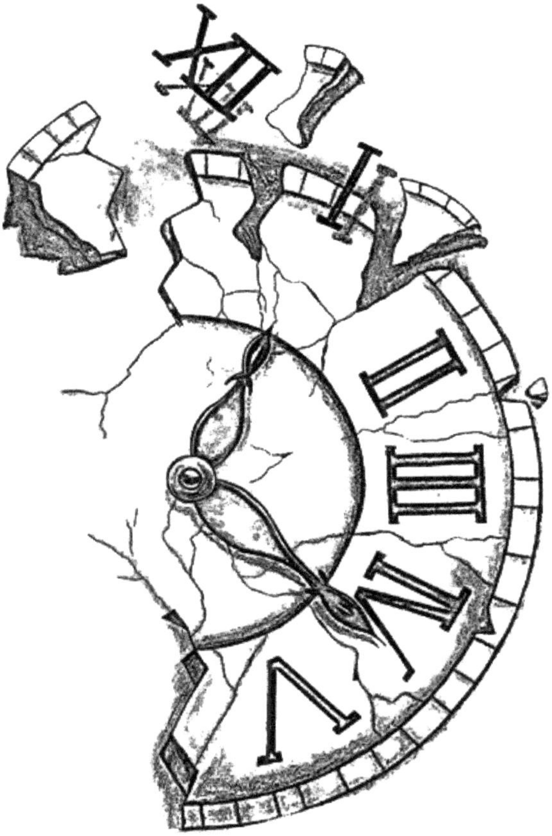

Clouds

I wish I could emulate the clouds up high,
As I observe their varied shapes, colors, and the sky.
A soft sigh escapes my lips, a wistful plea,
To see equality embraced, as it should be.

If only humanity could mirror the clouds above,
No fusing, no fighting, just unity, and love.
Clouds collaborate, in harmony they thrive,
Kindness doesn't weaken them; it makes them strong, alive.

Each cloud knows its role, its unique place,
Understanding the value of each step it takes.
If we were more like these clouds so wise,
Following our hearts, soaring in our own skies.

In our lanes, in our zones, we'd find our way,
No debates about who's right or wrong, day by day.
Just fulfilling our purpose, then moving on,
No judgment, no shame, just letting differences spawn.

Why do others insist on directing our lives?
Who gave them authority in these daily strives?

Let live and let live, accept diversity's song,
If we acted like clouds, we'd all get along.

Peace would descend, stress would decrease,
We'd find refreshment, and hearts would find ease.

Not giving what we
wouldn't wish to
receive,
We'd finally exhale,
and in unity, we'd
believe.
Breathe that sigh of
relief, let it be,
For if we were like the
clouds, our spirits
would be free.

Storms on the horizon

Shades of grey clouds blanket my skies

I must not let myself be discouraged

I will keep my eyes on the prize

I face many adversities by God's grace I rise

Sometimes these dark brown eyes cry

I can't afford to give up

I must continue on trying

I project my voice every time I speak

Today I thank my teacher Mr. Magee

For teaching me to make every word count each time I speak

I thank Mrs. Fears for helping me sharpen up my pen in creative writing

My pen is so cold you can feel the chills

It seemed like yesterday

I was playing with my cousins at grandma's house up the hill

My uncle Jesse telling me to turn that doggone music down

He loved his Old School Rhythm and Blues

He really could dance he knew how to get on down

You could feel the beat shake the ground

King Biscuit Blues Festival brought people from all over the world to Helena town

I know what it feels like to be misunderstood
When I was growing up, I was a young black boy in the hood
I never gave up I continued to follow my dreams
I refused to let anyone break my spirit or my self esteem
I'm still waiting for the day to come where
I get to entertain kings and queens
I remember when I was a fat kid with a
boom box like Radio Raheem
I'm capable of doing anything I put my
mind to do
I'll always cherish the day Mr. Langston
brought his band to Helena Crossing
Elementary School
I brought the house down I acted a fool
My life changed forever I went from being
a nerd to becoming mister cool
The journey of cultivating my voice has
been like the process of creating a
diamond under pressure
Preserving my family's legacy
I am a go getter
As life brings changes like the weather
Growing stronger and getting better
I will always remember the reason why I write

God willing, I will continue to rise

I refuse to let go of my dreams

I'm keeping my eyes on the prize.

The end.

About The Author

Edward Lee McDaniel Jr., known by the monikers Big Ed and MC. Lee, hails from Helena, Arkansas, where he delves into the art of poetry. His inspiration traces back to his father's recitation of Rudyard Kipling's "Gunga Din" during his formative years. With a captivating way with words, Edward clinched victories in numerous talent shows in his hometown and left an indelible mark in the open mic circuit and local talent scene in Memphis, Tennessee.

His poetic prowess has garnered attention on various platforms, including Radio Memphis Live Music Hour, Global Entertainment Network, Outlaw Radio, Dubceez Entertainment Network, and several other poetry podcasts like DSR Phull Purpoze Pens, Voices Behind The Pen, and Renaissance Poetry.

Finally, after much anticipation, Edward joyfully unveils his debut poetry book to the world, a realization of his lifelong dream. Join him as he leads you through the poetic expanse Beneath The Poet's Sky.

Printed in the USA
CPSIA information can be obtained
at www.ICGtesting.com
LVHW011237010224
770600LV00016B/130

9 787782 003900